Stardust Baby

Sara Jenkins

Grosvenor House
Publishing Limited

This book is published by
Grosvenor House Publishing Ltd
Link House
140 The Broadway, Tolworth, Surrey, KT6 7HT.
www.grosvenorhousepublishing.co.uk

A CIP record for this book
is available from the British Library

ISBN 978-1-78623-993-8

Acknowledgments:

Thank you a million times, Christine Amiss my super editor and advisor.
I couldn't have done this book without your expert advice and guidance.

Love to all my family you are forever in my heart.

This book is dedicated to Bob dog, William and all the star babies waiting to be born…

Stardust Baby avoids any reference to religious ideals or beliefs and equally makes no mention to discredit any religious groups. It is race, culture and religion neutral but has a distinct voice that children to which can relate.

Readers are encouraged to make *Stardust Baby* unique to their story, their own book. There is space for the reader to show their own creativity and imagination: to draw, colour, doodle or ponder thoughts. I have included some of my illustrations and doodles to complete the book.

Contents

Prologue

In our universe, far below the stars, here on planet Earth...
the wind blew,
ocean waves crashed,
rain poured,
rivers flowed.

In an English garden the roses swayed in the warm summer breeze. Bees buzzed
on cherry blossom trees, butterflies kissed lavender leaves, birds sang the sweetest of songs,
the air was filled with a delicate scent.

He breathed out, she breathed in;
We breath in, We breath out...

Once upon a time there was a family called Jenkins. They wanted to find a puppy dog to complete their family and they heard about a farmer who was selling his puppies. When the family went to the farm to find a puppy, Bob found them. The farmer put Bob in an old apple box and the family took him home.

What they didn't know then was that Bob was no ordinary dog and this is not just another dog story. This is a story about a dog, a baby and life: how to live it, how to love, how nothing new can start until something else ends and how to let go.

Bob was the sweetest, kindest being. Bob had some strange and somewhat funny ways and perhaps some might say he was a little odd!

The thing about Bob that not many people knew or understood was that Bob lived well and learnt how to live life. Bob understood the meaning and the mystery to life. Bob had learnt a lot and he would like to pass on his wisdom to you.

Every chapter is based on true events and includes a lesson Bob learnt. Hopefully his experiences may help you find your way through life...

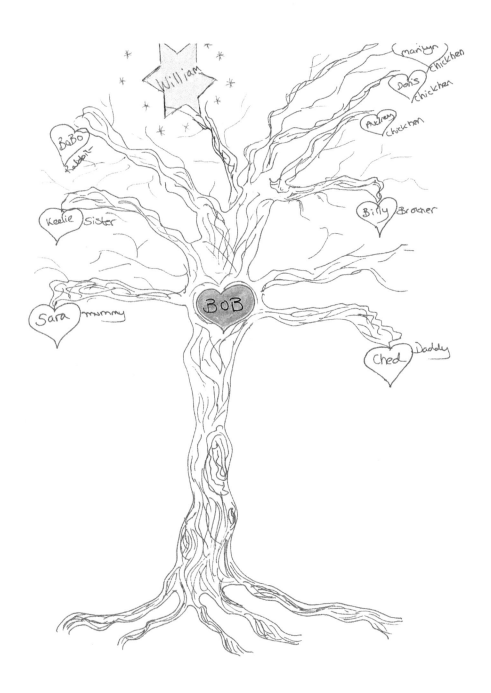

x

CHAPTER ONE:

The Stoop - Calmness

One of Bob's favorite past times was simply watching the world. Bob loved to sit on his 'stoop' – the top of the steps outside his front door. Bob had a fabulous view of the street up, down and opposite. Bob could pass many hours away watching and thinking or just watching. Bob liked to think this a good time to mediate on the meaning of life. Now we all now know and understand the benefits of meditation and how it works, we simply allow our thoughts to come and go through our minds. Scientists have researched the benefits of meditation and believe this helps our brains keep calm in anger and help us feel happier. How clever is that? All these benefits from just from sitting and letting our thoughts come and go!

Bob meditated best when the evenings were cool but warm enough to sit outside and the days were long and not getting dark until late into the evening. Bob observed many people pass by. The commuters off the train, some hurrying by, desperate to be home for dinner, others plodding slowly along chatting into those odd contraptions humans loved so much: mobile telephones. Bob thought these quite ridiculous! This need that humans had to be constantly doing, saying, something or other. He noticed they never actually saw the world around them and oh how much they missed.

Many of the commuters knew Bob and they did take time to stop and pat on his soft furry head and have a friendly chat as did the cheery postman who always made time for Bob asking how his day had been and in turn telling him about his day. The cheery postman told Bob all about how his job had changed. "A lot less letters. You see Bob, it's email now and parcels and packages from Internet shoppers. I tell you the World Wide Web has a lot to answer for, people can buy anything now and they do! Ordering stuff 24 hours' day and night. All this stuff makes my bag a lot heavier and I can tell you it's not good for a postman's back."

Bob always listened carefully and hoped he conveyed interest and kindness with his big soft brown eyes. Bob agreed with the cheery Postman about all his stuff people wanted. He noticed how many plates, cups and bowls his family had just sitting in cupboards. He had one bowl for water one and one for dinner so why they needed so many to stick in a cupboard was beyond him. They were the same with most things: clothes, shoes, books, bed stuff, cleaning stuff, houses were full of stuff that as far he could see mostly just sat unused and pointless or cluttered up the place causing them stress to take care of everything!

Bob knew humans only had two feet, one mouth and one bottom to sit on. Bob thought they could save themselves a lot of stress if they had less stuff to clean and care for. Why they couldn't see this was beyond him. As for this World Wide Web Internet thing, well this sounds like it has caused a lot of suffering for a lot of people. Bob had heard how bad things happen on this web thing. People really must be very careful on the Internet.

Bob watched the small people known as children passing to and from school. To be honest he found children all a bit full on for his taste with very frantic movements, squeals, sudden running actions, jumping and leaping about everywhere - it made his nerves bad. Couldn't a chap have a quiet moment on his stoop to meditate?

Now, dogs he fully understood. Bob noticed their behavior with intense observation. His nose would lift skywards feeling perhaps a little superior from his vantage point on the top step of the stoop where he enjoyed the last trace of their delightful aromas with utter contentment.

Bob was always curious. Well perhaps a bit nosey but being nosey is not such a bad thing it's just being interested in others. Being interested means we can learn stuff from others and that shows we care about them.

Besides learning from others Bob enjoyed just sitting in simple contemplation. He enjoyed the quiet times in between the busy commuters and dog walkers when all was still in the street. During these times, Bob, would empty his mind of thinking! Bob felt calm and his mind would become still thoughts drift in and drift out without him paying attention his mind was calm and relaxed free from thoughts and thinking.

Bob would observe the seasons as they started to change:

> the changing colors of the blossom trees in summer from bright vibrant green to deep darkest forest shades;

the leaves turning gradually from lush green to orange, bright like flames then darker auburn reds as the autumn leaves came to an end finally turning to crisp golden browns and falling down to earth below;

the roses fading in all their glorious colors losing their bloom, their petals falling to join the leaves below;

the birdsong changing as some birds migrated for the winter ahead to return the following spring.

Bob loved to watch the sky above, clouds that drifted by in fluffy, floating shapes free and wandering going wherever the wind blew them. The sky was a beautiful thing. Twilight, a special time from dusk to dark, showed the sky full of colors with purples, pinks, blues and oranges. The sun would set in the west and the moon would rise high above. Bob would sigh deeply feeling the earth settle to sleep around him with his mind still and his thoughts clear.

What did Bob learn?
Bob was interested in others. Bob gave others time to talk and he listened. He was curious about others and by being interested they knew he cared.

What was Bob doing?
Bob was resting his mind. He was not sleeping but his mind was taking a break from thinking. Bob took time to really notice the world where he lived.

Now have a think about yourself and ponder on these questions
How many colors can you see from your window or steps?
What helps you feel calm and peaceful?

CHAPTER 2

Dog Dancing – Euphoria

Oh yes! Dogs do love to dance as do many creatures!

Bob and his family loved to dance a lot. Sara and Keelie, who is Bob's human sister, loved to dance especially on Friday nights. They got up to some very crazy funny dancing. Bob always got rather over excited and too keen much to the annoyance it must be said of Keelie and Sara who, to be fair to Bob, took this Friday night dancing far too seriously!

Bob thought, "I don't care what they say. They're not stopping my dancing. I'm having a go and that's that!"

Bob would leap, spin and stand on his hind legs. Now let's be clear - Bob is very large Labrador dog. So dancing and prancing in a small living room means that a table, a TV and a dozen other breakable objects were all within a dog's tail swipe away from demolition. This posed somewhat of a challenge all round leading to the rather swift movement of objects out of the way of Bob's large tail. Fortunately for Bob his was always done successfully.

Bob did not give a fig how much space in the room he took. He just danced. Bob loved all music but he did favor Bob Marley who was in Bob's opinion the best Reggae musician the world had ever seen. Reggae music is the music of the Caribbean; of hot sunshine, crystal clear warm seas and the smell of coconuts, lime barbecue and jerk chicken.

Bob naturally assumed Bob Marley was named after him this made perfect sense to Bob. In Bob's opinion Bob Marley was a laid back, peaceful-living Jamaican singing and dancing around the world; Bob was a laid back, peaceful dog dancing in his living room. Bob (Dog not Marley ☺) had no rhythm, no actual dance steps or dance moves that could be identified. Did Bob care? No not at all, not in the slightest! He was lost in the moment of full throttle, 100% enjoyment.

For your information, Bob was named after Bobby Moore a very famous English football player.

Many years ago, Bobby Moore played football for a London club called West Ham United and went on to be captain of the English team that won the World Cup in 1966.

Dancing with others you love fills your heart full of joy. Sara and Keelie would laugh and dance pleading through their giggles, "Bob do let us have a turn! Watch us Bob."

Bob never did let them have a turn on their own. So, they all danced and sang to Bob Marley: Bob in his odd dog dancing way, Sara (who Bob thought was a worse dancer than he by a very long mile) and Keelie who did have rhythm and could actually produce recognizable dance moves. None of this mattered though because what did matter was dancing is fun, it's free and you can dance anywhere you want.

Dancing is great exercise for our bodies helping our hearts and lungs keep fit and healthy, making our leg muscles strong but most of all it's pure, utter fun! Dancing makes us smile. We feel good dancing, dancing, dancing, dancing, whether it's the funky chicken, the jive, the waltz, flamenco, salsa, foxtrot, rock and roll, line dance or "any old moves you want to make." People all over the world dance and have their own special dances for their cultures.

Anyone can dance - you move, you smile and you have fun. Try it alone in your room or with friends or even with dogs - just enjoy yourself. Who cares how good your moves are? Be like Bob and take up that space on the floor and dance. Bob thought everyone should dance more.

What did Bob learn?
Bob learnt that dancing doesn't hurt anyone. Only good things came from dancing if everyone in the world did a lot more dancing what a happier place the world would be...

Now think about yourself and have a ponder on these questions:
What is your favorite song that makes you jump and dance and sing for joy?
Who do think is a good dancer? Why?
What do you do for fun?

Dog Dancing

Go ahead and dance and smile and enjoy and have fun...

CHAPTER THREE:

Time to Taste – Appreciation

Food glorious food! Sweet, crunchy, smooth, hot, cold, spicy, tangy, sharp, fizzy, soft, mellow, hard, thick, cream, yummy in my tummy....

Bob was rather unusual for a Labrador as he wasn't much of a 'foodie' and he certainly wasn't greedy. This is odd for a Labrador as they are well known for excessive eating. Bob would turn his nose up to a sizzling sausage (Bob's human daddy Ched couldn't believe this. "What's wrong with this dog? What dogs don't eat sausages?" Bob didn't eat sweet treats and never begged the family for scraps or tidbits.

However, Bob had one weakness for a certain food and that was roast chicken. It was his favorite food in the universe. Bob did not gobble up his roast chicken. He would take his time to smell the lovely aroma and liked to admire how it looked. Bob would wait patiently for his dinner to cool to the right temperature, lick his lips, sit stand, sit stand all part of the ritual before he could start to eat his meal. Bob thought the contemplation before the eating was just as important and equally enjoyable. Finally, Bob would take a first, small tasty bite, thinking about the texture on his tongue and anticipating the explosion of juicy flavor. Every morsel was savored equally as the first; eating slowly and chewing carefully to the last bite was finished.

Even though Bob was not a 'foodie' he did try different foods having a nibble to taste new flavors. Bob surprised himself on a few occasions by liking things he didn't think he would for example; egg and cress sandwiches, cream, muffin cakes, cherry tomatoes, raw carrots, buttered toast, olives and grapes not a typical selection for dogs.

Bob noticed how a lot of creatures were always in a hurry eating. They stuffed anything they could grab into their mouths. "How could this be good for them?" thought Bob. "How did they ever taste anything? All that fast eating and stuffing faces, no wonder so many people and creatures alike had health problems." Bob would be grateful to his family for cooking his dinner and to the chicken for providing him with the food.

What did Bob learn?
Bob learnt to value and respect the chicken that gave him his favorite food. Bob thought the chicken deserved to have respect so he ate it mindfully showing his appreciation. Another good thing about being mindful of your food and eating slowly was that it took longer. You had more time to enjoy this lovely food.

Now think about yourself and ponder on these questions:
What is your favorite food?
How many chews can you take to eat something nice? Did that help you enjoy the food more?
How many words can you think to describe different types and flavors?
Be like Bob try something new you don't think you will like. You may be pleasantly surprised!

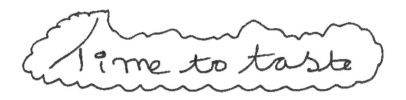

Time to taste

Bob enjoyed the taste a lot longer by practicing mindful eating.

Bob was a very smart dog indeed.

CHAPTER 4:

Chickens and Rabbits - Kindness

Bob was the kindest creature in many ways. Bob found being kind to others really took no effort at all. Bob would ponder on why would creatures choose to be unkind? Being unkind took far more thinking, effort and action thought Bob. This he believed took up valuable peace and tranquility.

So how then did Bob manage to be so kind all the time to all living beings? Perhaps this an example will explain.

Bob's human family (the Jenkins) on occasions would adopt poor unfortunate creatures in need of a good home love and kindness.

Bobo was the first adopted creature Bob encountered. Bobo first arrived one very cold, snowy December night the day before Christmas Eve. Bobo was a rabbit who was rescued from his wet, cold, and lonely outside hutch. Bobo was bought into the warm home of the Jenkins' family. Bobo was given a brand new Indoor hutch and was left in a quiet room overnight to adjust to his new hutch and environment.

Bob greeted this arrival with joy and enthusiasm, fanatically wagging his thick long tail! Bob was overcome with excitement. Now remember Bob was a dog and on occasion acted like a dog! Oh what joy! What a delight this was! How exciting with all the new smells.

Bob put his big furry dog head inside the hutch enthusiastically sniffing the fabulous new odors permeating up his nose! "Ahh hah," Bob thought, "a new creature, how delightful". Bob looked into the eyes of Bobo and thought "Oh dear what a poor bedraggled pitiful animal this is!" Bob realized this animal was down on his luck and in need of love kindness food and shelter.

Bob did not feel jealous or worried about this new creature coming to live with his human family, no not at all. Bob could see in Bobo's eyes a sad, scared, grumpy, angry rabbit looking back at him. "Poor Bobo," thought Bob, "what on earth has happened to this rabbit, has he never been cared for?" Bob felt nothing but kindness and compassion.

Little did Bob or Bobo realize this was just the start of the human family adopting creatures. It wasn't very long until the hens arrived. Now that was interesting! Bob being a dog found the hens utterly bewildering at first. The three hens were rescued from a battery egg farm. They arrived looking nothing like chickens they were scrawny and featherless not at all pretty looking hens to say the very least!

They were named Marilyn, Doris and Audrey, named somewhat ironically thought Bob, after three very beautiful actresses. Seriously who named chickens! Bob was bemused. This really was a challenge as Bob's favorite food was roast chicken and here were three pet hens to be loved, cared for and accepted. More than that, they were actually given equal status in the family. "Oh well, so be it" thought Bob. He must and will welcome these poor bedraggled hens into his home and garden and they would have a place in is heart too.

Bob had many delightful times sunbathing in his beloved garden with the hens scratching around him, occasionally jumping on his back or pecking his nose. Bob allowed this without even a grumble. He felt content to watch these odd hens scratch and peck. Bob loved to have a sniff as they roamed passed and much to his relief he noticed that they didn't smell like roast chicken.

What lesson do you think Bob learnt here?
Bob learnt how to accept creatures who were different to him. Bob learnt not to feel threatened by new creatures he did not understand. He learnt not to be jealous of sharing the love of his family with new creatures. By accepting others Bob gained new experiences. This included more animals to love and who loved him! Most surprising of all Bob realized that all these different creatures were not so different at all they all needed the same things he did.

Now have a think about yourself and ponder on these questions:
Who do you know that is different to you?
What have you learnt from them?
How are they like you?

CHAPTER 5

Perfect Poo – Respect

This chapter is of a rather more delicate, shall we say, personal nature, but I hasten to add a very important subject and something all living creatures must do! Poo of course. Now this was no laughing matter as far as Bob was concerned and taken very seriously indeed, because Bob did enjoy a good poo. It makes your tummy feels better afterwards more comfortable and of course space once again for food!

Bob would never poo in his own back yard, he was a very clean animal. Bob would like to take his time and with great care Bob would choose the right spot (up the park or in the woods on one of Bob's many walks) on where to do his poo.

This was at times a bit of a palaver and known to take quite a time (much to the impatience of the human out with him) as Bob searched for the exact spot to have a perfect poo. This ritual would take considerable sniffing of trees, grass and all the plant life in the area; a rummage with a lot of turning and swirling until finally a selection would be made (hallelujah! the humans would say). Finally, Bob would plant his bottom ready for action only to have a change of mind - no not good enough- then up bottom and off he would go searching once more. He stopped at several test sites along the way, a wee here and there, to check if they were suitable for Bob's required needs. Eventually a perfect spot would be found, usually behind a tree or bush. Bob valued his privacy as most creatures do when having a poo and using the bathroom is a rather personal task after all. Obviously when we are young we need help with our bathroom activities. There comes a time when you will no longer need any help with washing or using the toilet therefore it is important that your privacy is respected. You will know when the time is right for you.

So, having a poo is a natural process and if we eat healthy looking after our insides, our bodies get all the goodness we need from our food. Our bodies, being very clever, get rid of the rubbish we don't need and makes our poo.

Our bodies need food for fuel just like motor cars need oil to make them work. We need the right food to make our bodies work well. Our food should not have too much sweet, sugary stuff. Sweet treats should be treats. We need lots of tasty vegetables & fruit too with enough protein and other varied foods, good things like olives and almonds. Not forgetting treats like cake - this is OK too sometimes. We must have respect for our lovely bodies because it is where 'WE' live! Our body is our shell so it's up to us to take good care of our own body.

Food is fuel and our bodies turn the rubbish bit into poo. So going to the toilet is very important for keeping our bodies healthy. We also need to make sure we keep clean too just like Bob. Babies should learn to use a potty, Bob couldn't understand why humans waited to start to teach babies how to use the potty until they were 2 years old. To Bob this simply didn't make sense because puppies, kittens and bunnies are taught toilet training and how to use the litter tray from a very, very early age just a few weeks old. Bob had observed in his human family they practiced this early toilet training with their babies and animals and it seemed to work for them.

It's important for creatures and us to feel safe and comfortable so they will enjoy having a good poo (some humans like reading when on the toilet). After each poo you will feel nice and clean - not just your bottom and tummy - but we must always keep our potties clean and wash our hands very well with lots of soap an water afterwards. We then feel healthy, clean and refreshed.

You see things have an order so we should complete each phase of the process to enable us to move on to the next part:

Food = Fuel
Fuel = Energy for living and learning
Poo = Rubbish the body doesn't need.

All living things need the same basic things to thrive, to live healthy and to grow. When we have enough food, shelter, warmth and feel clean we are ready to learn to move on to the next phase. Then we can grow and respect our bodies, hearts and minds.

What lesson did Bob learn?

Bob learnt we have basic needs to be met. It is important to take care of and pay attention to our bodies 'our shell'.

Now have a think about yourself and ponder on these questions:

What makes you feel nice and clean?

How do you take care of your body?

What makes you feel ready to go on to the next phase? Perhaps it's bath time then bedtime breakfast before school?

Maybe you can start to make a list of things that can help you get started everyday...

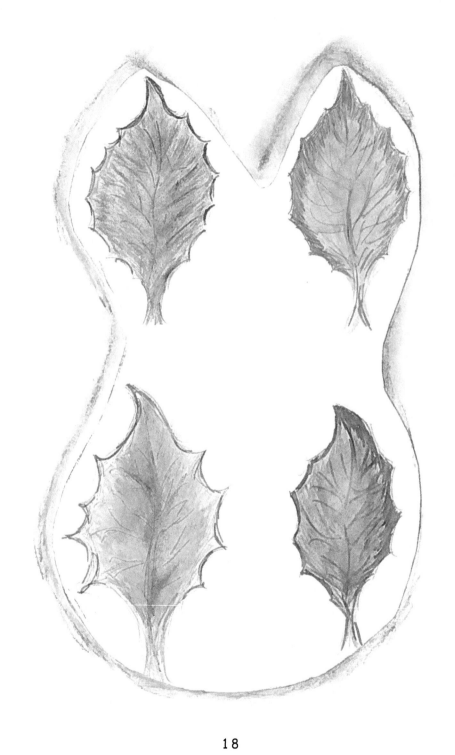

CHAPTER 6

Ballet Legs - Trust

Bob liked to stretch his legs and point his toes in the most perfect ballet pose. Now of course being a dog with paws this took lots of practice (practice is something we shall discuss later). Even Bob with his amazing status needed a little helping hand with perfecting his technique.

Now this is important so listen very carefully...you will need to practice good listening skills. Good listening is paying attention completely and fully without interruption to what another person is trying to say. You listen with your ears and you listen with your heart. Then you will truly understand what the person, creature or being is really saying.

No creatures or beings are ever able to do everything alone. Knowing when and how to ask others to help you is a very important life lesson we all must learn. If you ask for help you are not saying "I am useless." No, no, no you are simply saying, "I am a humble being that is not too proud or too stubborn to ask for help."

When we ask another being for help, we get our much-needed assistance from others. They in turn get to feel good to be asked for help they feel proud and kind that they have helped you. They feel warm to you because you are showing others who you really are. You are allowing others to see you are vulnerable and this makes others feel closer to you as they 'know who you really are'. The others feel happier because you have made them feel good about themselves and they feel helpful, useful and kind. Oh my what power you have over others by just being honest and humble about who you really are.

Now we have spoken about the lesson learnt I hear you wondering what has this to do with ballet, what help and by whom? Uncle Billy is the 'who'. Uncle Billy was also Bob's non-furry human brother (ummm yes all gets a bit complicated I know but bear with us keep reading... all becomes clear). We shall refer to him simply as Bill.

Bill with great kindness and patience would massage Bob's hard working furry legs, paws and toes. Bill would use his big, strong warm hands to rub Bob's aching muscles. Billy always did this for Bob after a walk, especially as he aged and needed extra care for his poor old legs. This helped Bob to unwind and relax. With the warmth of touch and the kindness of Bill, Bob would feel the heat healing right down through to his bones. Bob would trust Bill entirely. Bill would gently help Bob stretch his legs right down to the tips of his toes pointing them in a perfect ballet point. This practice occurred most evenings and was a mutual enjoyment for both. They both felt loved by the other and the practice helped Bob's old legs considerably. There was of course a by-product to this practice (much to the dismay of human mother Sara) and that was there was enough fur shed on the floor to make another dog!

What lesson did Bob learn?
Bob learnt how to ask for help and how to trust another to help him. Bob knew he needed help to achieve his ballet legs stretches. Bob also, rather surprisingly he thought, learnt how allowing others to help helped the other person just as much!!!!

Now have a think about yourself and ponder on these questions:
When did you ask for help and how did this feel?
Did you notice how the other person felt as well? Did you feel better after you asked for help?

Use this space to color in or draw....

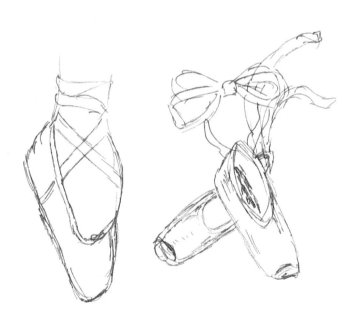

21

Chapter 7

Golf and Goats – Assumptions.

Bob enjoyed his walks! He frequented many parks in his local area and was indeed a well-known figure amongst his fellow dog walking community. Bob's favourite spot was the local Golf Course - well the wood and grass area to the side to be precise. However, there is not a gate, fence or wall to separate these two areas and this is important for our story

It was a bright Autumn morning still sunny and warm. Bob and Mummy Sara went for a nice pleasant morning stroll. Side by side they walked along in companionable silence. Sara admiring the beautiful colors of the Autumn trees and thinking all the while about enjoying a nice hot cup of coffee afterwards. Bob blissfully sniffing blades of grass one at a time (a very time consuming habit this was) and stopping at every tree trunk, shrub and bush in his path, to do what dogs like to do… pee of course! Both were content minding their own business.

After some time and some way into their walk they were greeted with a dreadful smell, a stink like nothing else they had smelt before. It was awful. Bob was completely befuddled by this odor and he jumped up and down, growled, sniffed in circles. Bob started to bark loudly looking up a tree. "What on earth was going on with Bob?" thought Sara. Bob was not a dog who would behave in this manner as he found barking and growling quite unseemly.

Soon everything became clear. High up a tree standing on a large branch eating leaves was a huge Goat. The Goat became extremely excited at the sight of Sara and Bob. The Goat happily climbed down from his perch up the tree and it must be said he was very pleased to see them. Bob had never met a goat before so meeting another unknown creature at his local park was unexpected and rather a fright. This was a creature that really did smell different and Bob didn't quite know what to make of this animal. Bob, being Bob, knew to be kind to new creatures no matter how different to him they appeared to be. Bob realized this Goat (apparently, that was what it was according to his Mummy) was lost and scared. "This goat is in the wrong place," thought Bob. Goats don't go for walks at parks and they don't live here – that much he did know.

Bob and Sara looked at each other "Well Bob we'd better go back to the car park and I'll pop in the golf club office and tell them what we have found," said Sara. Sara always talked to Bob in fact all his family enjoyed engaging him in conversations and would, often ask his opinion and advice. Of course, Bob couldn't speak but never the less they understood perfectly what the other was thinking and saying.

But the Goat had other plans! He had taken a shine to Sara and Bob and off he went following after them.

"Oh dear" thought Bob, "This Goat is following us."
"Oh dear" thought Sara. She said "Bob let's walk faster and hope we can lose him. Come on let's get to the office as quick as we can."
On they went in a brisk walking pace.
Another dog walker passing by shouted at them, "You can't walk goats here you know!"
Flabbergasted Sara replied, "Excuse me you silly a woman. He is not my goat! I'm not walking a goat he's following us. Obviously he's been abandoned here and needs help!"

The woman dog walker stuck her nose in the air not convinced Sara was not walking the Goat and clearly had no concern for the lost animal. The dog walker stormed off.

Onwards they continued, Bob, Sara and the Goat, towards the golf course office. Once again, their journey was interrupted, "Oi you get your Goat off the golf course. I've had enough of you people and your Goats!".

At this Sara came to a full stop thrust her hands-on hips and turned to face the man on the golf course. "Oh oh" thought Bob "I've seen that look on her face - here comes trouble! Time to hide behind a tree."

Sara was very, very, cross. Angry would probably be the best description. Sara had an extremely loud voice like a bellow or a foghorn. Oh boy when she shouted the earth literally shook beneath our feet and paws. Sara exploded, "You what! You silly man I'm fed up with this I'm not walking a Goat. He's not my Goat its lost, scared and abandoned. He needs help!"

At this the man drew a hasty retreat. No way was he sticking around to hear such nonsense. He stuck his nose in the air threw back his shoulders and sauntered off to play his golf.

Finally after a fraught walk, the golf course office and car park were in sight. Quickly Bob made a hasty run and with relief jumped into the boot of the car pleased his part of this adventure with the Goat had come to an end.

Sara popped into the office to find a chap reading his paper minding his own business. "Excuse me there's a Goat outside, a rather large Goat actually the size of a horse. The Goat has followed me and my dog Bob."

At this interruption, the chap, looked up none too bothered " Arrrh another one!"
Rather surprised by his reaction this wasn't what Sara expected.
"Another one? What do mean there's more?" Sara enquired.

The man closed and folded his newspaper and picked up a sturdy looking rope. "Oh yes seems someone or some people drop off these poor fellows. These Goats get too big and eat everything in sight. Folks don't realize how much care Goats need you see, so they leave them here. Thing is it's not right but people don't always know where or who to turn to for help they just drop them here in a panic. Don't worry luv I'll get him and call the National Society for Goat Rescue and Rehabilitation for the south-east and north Kent region. People don't know about the goat rescue society you see."

Sara felt reassured she had found someone to help with her Goat problem. Sara was happy and relieved to know the Goat would be rescued and go to an appropriate place where he could live happily and be properly cared for.

Bob thought about the Goat and how lost and scared he must have felt. Bob thought about the people who had left the Goat there too and how similar they must have felt not knowing what to do, who or where to turn. How easily people get in a muddle and make judgments of each other without really understanding what was going on. Wouldn't it be nicer for everyone if they just communicated better?

What lesson can we learn here?

Bob learnt about how people make judgments about others and assume 'something is something' when in fact they are misinformed.

Bob learnt that we should remember to keep an open mind and think before we act on impulse

Now have a think about yourself and ponder on these questions:

Have you assumed something about another person only to find out the things you thought about then, turned out to be very different?

Space to colour, draw and ponder your thoughts...

Golf & Goats.

gave This adventure some
contemplation and decided
although new creatures
were different that was
fine different creatures were
interesting after all and
all similar to. they all need
a home food water and to be
loved and looked after
how lucky Bob felt thinking
about his warm home, cosy
bed and loving human family

Bob wished the goat
the very same...

CHAPTER 8

Showtime - Fear

A storm is nature showing us a spectacular firework display. Mother Nature is having fun putting on a show and thoroughly showing off in the process. She's getting rid of some pent-up energy and having a party. Now sometimes because Mother Nature is having such a good time she does get a bit carried away and causes a bit of a mess!

Bob was very, very, very frightened of thunder and lightning. The thunder would rumble overhead in the dark sky, like a very big angry animal growling. The noise would be so loud that the house would shake and the floor would move beneath our feet and his paws. As with a growling sound coming nearer there would be a CRACK and a THWACK and a BANG and a THUMP! Then the sky would light up with the brightest white. The lightning would dance zigzagging across the dark sky lighting it white and electric blue. Mother Nature can get very excited at her abilities to perform! She sometimes forgets that many beings and creatures below her have a rough time feeling scared and worried about all this noise and commotion.

Bob was indeed one of these creatures having a particularly difficult time. Bob had no idea what this storm business was all about. He did not realize it was just Mother Nature putting on a show and well, quite frankly, just being a show off. Bob thought something bad was coming to get him. Bob was, as you know, a very large furry yellow Labrador. While the storm raged high above his ears, Bob tried desperately to hide from this scary thing outside. Bob would run from room to room searching desperately for a safe place. "Ah hah" he thought, "under the bed I will go." Now this very large Labrador dog would try to squeeze himself under a one-inch gap. Ridiculous! Not even the tip of his nose would fit!

As Bob's pursuit for safety continued Bob would spin in circles finally jumping on a human's lap, which I must say, was a challenge. The poor dear humans did try to entertain this behavior especially human mummy Sara who secretly yearned for this lap sized creature to join her. Bob would be comforted and cuddled and soothed with reassuring words. Mummy would explain to Bob "It's just Mother Nature having a party and she's a real show off, isn't she? Don't worry you are safe. The storm will soon stop. Mother Nature will get tired and go to sleep."

Being comforted in his time of need, Bob realized things that seem scary often cannot hurt us; however, we must have respect for Mother Nature because she is very powerful.

During these storms, Bob was of course safe in his lovely cozy home. Bob decided that it is OK to be scared sometimes and it is helpful when we feel scared to talk about our fears with someone we trust. Bob found great comfort with his human mummy Sara who would calmly explain to Bob what was happening outside. Bob realized having someone to talk to him helped him discover what scared him. Finding out more about what scared him helped him understand and ease his fears about storms.

Bob understood that people and creatures alike have many fears. He knew when Billy was small he was very scared of the dark. Bob being a dog thought this was daft because he had good night vision and could see clearly in the dark. He knew there was nothing to fear. Bob remembered Sara telling Billy that the dark was just the world going to sleep as the sun was closing its eyes and sleeping. Bob thought that made perfect sense because when he closed his eyes it was dark! There was nothing to fear. It was all in his imagination.

So what did Bob learn from this?
Bob learnt that when feel scared about something it helps to share it with another person. It's OK to be scared sometimes because we all are scared at times. Learn about the thing that scares you, respect it and try to understand it more so you can feel better about your fears just like Bob and his storms.

Now have a think about yourself and ponder on these questions:
What scares you and how can you find out more about it?
Who can you talk to when you are feeling afraid about something or someone?

CHAPTER 9

Dipping In – Safety

Swimming! What a joy, what a pleasure! Oh how Bob loved to swim!

Bob would swim in all weathers; hot, cold, rain, wind, even snow (if he'd been allowed). Bob would swim in any water, sea, river, lakes and pools. Bob wouldn't hesitate - he would be straight in and off he went.

Bob had many adventures that involved swimming. The first dip in the sea was on a lovely summer's day. Off he went in the car to the seaside. Upon arrival, he was beside himself with excitement. He could see this large expanse of water and smell new aromas in the air so off he went leaping and bounding with his large furry tail wagging. Bob enjoyed drinking the sea water as he swam (*now this is something all humans should never do*).

Yuck, yuck, yuck, cough splutter, cough splutter! "What, what, is this water? This sea stuff tasted ghastly" thought Bob. The family very worried and bemused why he would try to drink sea water. Doesn't everyone know you can never drink sea-water as it is full of salt?

Bob had never seen the sea and so no, he did not know this. They offered Bob fresh clean water to drink to ease his sore throat. Bob however was having none of it and thought, "I'm not drinking anything away from home. Oh no I don't want any more of that sea water stuff. No thank you."

Bob learnt a valuable lesson: don't trust something is OK just because it looks the same. Bob never drank the sea again but he did enjoy many swims in the sea. Bob wasn't put off and he thought that just because something didn't go well the first time you can try it again. Bob's advice is don't be put off something if at first all does not go well. Have another go before you decide it's not for you.

Another of Bob's favorite places to swim was a local lake in the middle of a beautiful natural meadow. This area was a safe haven and home to lots of wildlife. Generally, everyone got on well coexisting and enjoying the lake and meadow. All the creatures knew their place and respected everybody else. However, Bob assumed on this sunny afternoon that he was perfectly in his rights to enjoy his swim in the cool, green, calm waters of the lovely lake. Just, what he needed on a hot day a refreshing swim to cool his hot furry body. Run, jump, splash in he went. "Ah bliss" he thought, swimming along minding his own business paying no attention to the fish beneath his paddling paws, unaware of the strikingly electric blue dragon flies dipping and swooping into the water to drink, or even noticing a family of ducks swimming contentedly in the water..

Suddenly a frantic commotion started nearby when a very, very, large mother Swan saw Bob heading in what she thought was her direction to get her babies called 'signets'. Being a new mother, Swan was fiercely protective of her signets and she must have felt afraid and threatened. Mother Swan took off into the air her huge wings flapping faster and faster. She flew up just above the lake and she swooped and swished her wings furiously at Bob's head trying to push him under the water. Bob was totally taken by surprise! He hadn't seen her as he was so intent on getting into the lovely cool lake he hadn't taken the time to STOP! LOOK! CHECK! Was it safe to swim? Mother Swan didn't understand Bob had no intention of hurting her signets - all she thought was they are in danger. Of course, we all know Bob would never hurt another living creature but she didn't understand this as she didn't know anything about him.

It was Bob who was in danger; Bob swam frantically, paws peddling full dog power. Bob realized his mistake when he spotted three brown signets clucking and wings splashing nearby. Bob understood what was happening "Ah hah she's afraid. They're all afraid! Silly me I should know better than go near frightened creatures that do not understand I mean no harm."

Bob turned around and swam in the opposite direction. Bob reached the safety of the river bank and dragged himself out, fully out of breath, rather shaken but otherwise unharmed. Mother Swan settled back on the lake with signets safely beside her. Bob's family were all relieved to have him safely back and agreed they all must be careful in future to make sure it is safe for Bob to go swimming.

What did learn Bob from this incident?
Bob learnt swimming is a wonderful thing to do and we all should learn to swim and enjoy the water. Water is fun but we must ALWAYS check it is safe to swim.

Now have a think about yourself and ponder on these questions:
How do you feel about swimming and getting into the water?
What do you do when you feel that something might put you in danger?
Have you ever felt out of your depth when you tried something new? How did that feel?

Use this space to draw, wonder, write, your thoughts and feelings…

CHAPTER 10

Duvet Comfort – Peace

The perfect place to sleep consists of a warm, soft cozy duvet with clean, crisp bed linen and a mattress soft as a marshmallow so that you sink in and float away on a blissful cloud of soft comfort. One of Bob's favourite pastimes was to sink onto his bed and sleep. That was wonderful!

A sleep can be taken when or wherever conveniently safe to do so. Bob enjoyed many 'cat naps' - nothing to do with cats and the only connection to this phrase as far as Bob could fathom was cats enjoyed sleep more than he did. They managed to partake in these 'cat naps' just about anywhere at any time!

A 'cat nap' simply explained is a sleep taken anytime from waking up in the morning to before going back to sleep for the night. This rather luxurious pastime can take place anywhere that is safe to do so: in arm chairs, on sofas, in cars (obviously if you are not the driver), trains, planes, on the grass, in parks or gardens, on a sun lounge (Sara's favorite.) Well that's a long list of places to catnap.

Relaxing and sleeping is not only a pleasure but essential for our physical and mental wellbeing. Sleep gives us energy to run, jump, play, learn and laugh. A very important chapter and lesson Bob learnt is that a good sleep helps us grow and learn. Without sleep we simply cannot learn or function properly. Sleep helps the body repair itself, allows us time to grow and gives our minds a rest from all our thinking and doing. Plus, when we are tired we don't enjoy ourselves. We stop being able to have fun and miss out on lots of good things. Sometimes we must practice sleep and teach ourselves how to sleep properly, how to turn off our thinking and stop our doing.

Bob observed many different creatures sleeping. He noticed birds just needed a tree branch or a few twigs to make a nest, nothing fancy. Cats, well they would just curl up anywhere like near a wall, a step, a bit of concrete. Cats had a knack for finding a safe spot out of the wind, not too hot, or cold and just nap. Bob knew that not all people or creatures had a perfect, comfy soft bed to sleep in. He also knew that creatures can make a bed and sleep pretty much anywhere. They just had to make do and realize the important part is … well the sleeping!

Sleep is our friend and like lots of other things we must learn to be good at it and practice. Bob wondered why some creatures struggled with getting enough sleep. Perhaps they thought they will miss out on something? Others might fear what happens when we sleep.

Bob knew you miss out far more not getting enough sleep and being too tired to do anything properly wasn't any good at all. Bob also knew that our bodies take great care of us when we sleep and go into 'auto pilot'. Our bodies take care of our needs for us without us having to think about it. Well now how clever is that!

An extra bonus we have is those lovely dreams of warm sunny places. Bad dreams were just that - bad dreams go away as soon as we wake up. Nothing at all to be scared of at all (remember always tell someone you trust if something scares you even a dream.) So you see everything about sleep is a good thing and even better if you master the skill of naps - a pleasure Bob highly recommends and Bob will concede even cats are great at this!

What lesson did Bob learn?
Bob learnt that ultimately it's not what your bed is like, or even a bed at all that's important, but the result the sleep part is all that really matters.

Now have a think about yourself and ponder on these questions:
How do you feel when you wake up in the mornings?
Where is your best sleeping place? Where do you like to take a nap?
Why do you think some people have trouble sleeping?

CHAPTER 11

Paws Over Ears - Emotions

Bob did not do shouting, barking, growling or any such poor behavior. Bob kept a calm mind and body always. Bob lived with a very crazy, odd, shouting, bonkers human family. Despite this Bob loved his family and felt only compassion for them and wished them nothing but kind thoughts.

Bob noticed how they would get upset and angry at so many things. Often these things causing them so much anxiety were silly, small and insignificant in the great scheme of life!

Bob noticed that all this shouting and anger never made any of them feel better. They never resolved anything so there would be more shouting and more anger. They couldn't see how bad this behavior was for all of them and they couldn't stop it either. Bob would sigh and think, "Uh oh here we they go again these poor dear silly people."

Bob felt helpless to help them. He would breath in and breath out trying to keep his mind calm in the hope his calmness would somehow pass on to them. When the crazy shouting was too much Bob would put his paws over his ears to block out their racket. Sometimes however even this wasn't enough so Bob did what all smart creatures do - he would stand up and remove himself from this behavior around him. Funnily enough the family always seemed to notice this. "Now look what you've done even the dog wants to leave the room!" one of them always shouted. So, the silly people would shout even more blaming each other for shouting!

Sooner or later someone would jump up, shout the loudest and open the door for Bob letting him escape to the quiet space in the porch. Bob would leave the room and all the shouting would continue but this time it was all about Bob and the original argument forgotten. Now they were all upset because "Even the dog had to leave the room!"

"Such silly people" thought Bob. He was in despair feeling nothing but compassion for them. He saw how stressed they became and how out of control they felt. Bob would look at them with kindness.

If Bob could speak he would have been speechless at this! Bob would lay in favorite spot the one without central heating as Bob had a substantial fur coat. He was rather grateful for the cold air especially when the tempers in the house became so hot.

Bob could see the family through the glass door. Eventually the shouting would stop with nothing ever resolved. No one even knew who started the argument or what it was all about. The only thing Bob could see was that that they were all upset and angry and they never seemed to learn or change their behavior. Bob thought, "Why don't they speak calmly to each other and talk about how they felt? Instead of all this accusing and angry shouting?"

Bob could see and hear they were clearly telling each other they were upset. However they would get a better result if they spoke instead of shouting at each other. Then they wouldn't get so upset about how they were feeling and this would help them they listen better too."

This always left Bob feeling completely and utterly baffled. Bob noticed that people who spoke about their feelings 'openly' telling each other about their different emotions appeared to be a lot closer to each other and a lot happier. He knew from his own experience that the more people talked and shared their feelings the more they understood how and why they felt the way they do. Bob heard them talk about their emotions: sad, excited, overwhelmed, mad, glad, bad, disappointed, frustrated, lost, lonely, happy. These were just some of the expressions people used when talking about how they felt. Bob thought this was a good start to the emotions list and he had felt these at emotions at times and indeed many more.

As far as Bob could fathom Anger is a reaction to being upset about something or feeling that you have been hurt. Bob knew that when people took the 'angry bit' or the 'snap and snarl bit' out of their words they usually got a better response and felt better. Words can hurt people's feelings and make people feel bad as well.

What did Bob learn?

Bob once heard a wise man say of Anger, "It is like holding a burning piece of coal in your hand. It only hurts you, burning your hand and your heart. It keeps you stuck in your hurt so you're thinking sticks to this pain and the more upset you become. That burning coal stops you thinking calm and clear thoughts so put the coal down."

Now think about yourself and ponder on these questions:

Bob describes anger like "holding a hot piece of coal." How would you describe the feeling of anger?

What makes you feel angry or upset?

What do you do to make yourself feel better? Or the person you have hurt?

How many more emotions can you name?

Is there a feeling that perhaps you think you might hide?

Paws or Ears

burning in your heart it only
hurts you and it keeps you
from thinking nice calm thoughts

CHAPTER 12

Feet for Paws - Empathy

Bob had paws and his paws were his feet.

Bob had issues with his feet/paws. This was rather intriguing to Bob because he was by his very nature a very controlled sensible creature. However, this odd issue with his feet/paws has baffled Bob for many years...

Bob, as we know, loved to be touched by all other living creatures. Being stroked, cuddled and massaged all bought great joy and pleasure; yet Bob could not bear to have anyone touch his feet/paws.
Not all!
Not even in the slightest bit…
Not by absolutely anyone …
Not even his beloved family.

The mere mention of a toenail trim would bring about frantic hysteria and manic jumping up and down. Panic ensued at a mere flick of toe, Bob would leap onto all four feet/paws, jig and dance, tummy flipping, heart racing, teeth on edge! Bob was puzzled, he thought, "This is quite ridiculous! Absurd! What is this all about?"

Bob spent many hours pondering the meaning of this trying to fathom why this happened. Stoop time was a spot for such contemplation. On one of these occasions Bob felt totally attuned (tuned in to how another is thinking and feeling) to his Mummy Sara and had a sudden clarity of thought.

Bob had great depth of feeling and understanding for his family. He understood their feelings, their emotions and their behavior. Bob had empathy for his family. Empathy is when we put our 'feet' literally into the shoes of others, we are not feeling sorry for them - this is much more. We try to understand how they are feeling, to see the world through their eyes and to think what it feels like to them.

One warm sunny day, not too hot just the perfect temperature; Bob was snoozing on the stoop. Bob lay relaxing in the pre-twilight sunshine every so often glancing at Sara pruning her beloved English roses. Bob was eye level to her feet he noticed she was wearing her favorite foot wear flip-flops (a Brazilian brand). As she pruned away the flip-flops flapped making that flip flop familiar sound. It was the sound of the flip-flop that caught Bob's attention. Bob couldn't help but look at her feet; Bob's attention was thoroughly focused on her feet. Bob really, really, looked and that Sara's feet had a rather funny, misshapen, odd look for a human. One was smaller and thinner, one was bigger and fatter and a bit twisty inwards not particular good for walking about on. "Hmm that looks rather uncomfortable," thought Bob.

Bob knew Mummy Sara had trouble with her feet and she could only wear certain footwear. She had a lot of pain and discomfort she could not stand or walk for long. Because Bob was a very attentive good listener, he knew that she was born with a disability of her feet. Somehow her feet were not born the way they should have been.

With deep compassion and empathy for his beloved Mummy Sara on that sunny afternoon, Bob literally stood in Sara's feet and he felt her pain and suffering with such a deep understanding. Bob thought, "Ah-ha she has a foot phobia like me! Now I know why she is so sensitive about her feet being touched. My poor dear Mummy Sara had operations to help her walk and still suffers with pain and discomfort but it's the left-over anxiety that disturbs her the most, therefore she has developed a toenail foot phobia."

Bob decided he could help himself and Mummy Sara by being a role model on toenail foot phobia. Bob would show his Mummy Sara that calm thoughts and breathing exercises would help them both to reduce and control their panic and anxiety. Bob felt content with this idea. He smiled (oh yes dogs do smile) and dozed off to sleep to the smell of grass, lavender and the sound of bees buzzing, birds singing, clippers clipping English roses and flip flops flapping.

What did Bob learn?
Bob learnt that understanding our fears was a step to coming to terms with them. Bob also learnt that when you 'walked in someone's shoes' you might see things from their perspective and that will help you understand them better.

Now think about yourself and ponder on these questions:
What do you think empathy is?
When have you felt empathy for someone and 'walked around in their shoes'?
Is there someone you feel has empathy for you?
Who do you know that has a disability? How do you react around that person?

CHAPTER 13

The One - Love

The One? Who or what is The One?

The One was Bob's person (any living creature can be The One and all living creatures have a desire a need to have The One). Bob's very special person was his human daddy Trevor, affectionately known as Ched.

Bob loved all his family, creatures and beings on earth but Bob had his very special bond with Ched. Bob knew in his heart that Ched would be thinking about him during the day when Bob was home alone. Ched would be busy at work building houses for people to live. Bob would 'think' about his Ched he would feel warm inside and knew Ched would be thinking fondly of him. Knowing this made Bob feel, safe, secure and loved. The days at home could be long and lonely for Bob. While his family was all out doing human stuff, "Goodness knows what," thought Bob, he never felt all alone he could feel they were with him somewhere deep inside of him. Bob knew they felt the same especially his Ched. Bob was being carried in his Ched's heart and this was always a very reassuring feeling so Bob never felt truly alone.

When Ched, came home from building houses he always insisted on taking Bob for a walk even if he had just had a walk with someone else in the family. Ched insisted on going for his walk with his beloved Bob Dog. Off they would go to enjoy their quiet time walking side by side. Bob knew how special this time was to them both. Ched needed his 'space', his time out to de-stress after a busy day's work, with his best friend his dog Bob'. They would return home with clear minds and hearts full of love.

Bob enjoyed his walks with all his family but Bob knew that there was something different about his walks with Ched. Often upon their return Ched would settle in his most comfortable armchair ready to relax for the evening and enjoy watching his favorite television programs. Bob who cared nothing for the moving pictures and talking square box called a television thought it was another odd contraption. Humans watched a lot of television and they often got upset or scared at what they saw. Television kept the little people awake at night making them tired for school the next day. Oh my, the time they wasted sitting on their bottoms watching a square box! They could be doing something much more useful or doing fun things like reading books, painting pictures, dancing, walking, learning how to cook a real healthy meal from scratch. Bob simply couldn't fathom these people out.

Ah yes now back to Ched and Bob. Ched was content to watch his television. While he was happily pursuing, this Bob would settle himself on the rug in front of Ched's chair. Bob would feel so much love kindness and compassion for his One, his very special Ched. Bob just felt utterly overwhelmed with his feelings of goodness for Ched that he would be beside himself and get rather too excited in his devotion. Bob would sit up and stare at Ched not moving an inch not blinking, just simply staring!

Ched found all this a bit too full on and at times didn't really know how to respond to all this devoted attention. Ched would say to Sara "What does he want? What am I to do now? He's had his walk, his dinner and a cuddle why does he keep staring at me? If I make eye contact ,even the slightest glance of eyeball, he's going to do that leaping up crazy dancing stuff." Bob would interpret this minuscule glance and the conversation with Sara as a clear signal to do just that! Up he would jump, large fury tail enthusiastically wagging, two front paws doing a wonderful interpretation of a horse doing dressage.

Sara found this very amusing. She was left to sit peacefully watching the television Sara would giggle and reply, "Well Ched he just loves you. He just wants to tell you how much he loves you and how special you are to him. He is most attached to you. I'm afraid you're The One. How lucky you are."

Ched would sigh, smile and pat Bob fondly on his big soft furry head. Ched's kind loving blue eyes would look into Bob's chocolate brown eyes both feeling connected and loved. Despite all their funny and annoying ways they loved each other deeply.

Bob thought, "Yes, yes, yes. Of course, it's love without words. It's that special bond between us. We have it and it is always there even when I can't see you. I love you and you love me. We both know this and we both feel the same."

What did Bob learn from this?

Bob learnt that everyone should have someone special in their lives they call The One. It may or may not be someone in your family but someone who will do anything for you. It is Some-one who has you and your best interests in their heart.

Now think about yourself and ponder on these questions:

Who do you fondly think about when you at school? Who is your One?

Who do you think might think about you a special person? This might be a parent, a friend, a relative, a teacher or someone else you might know or even a pet like Bob?

Think about your One and how you feel when you can't see them. Describe your feelings perhaps using colors may help.

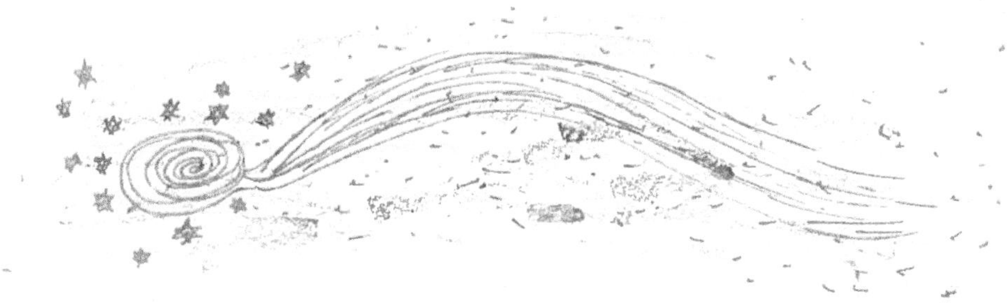

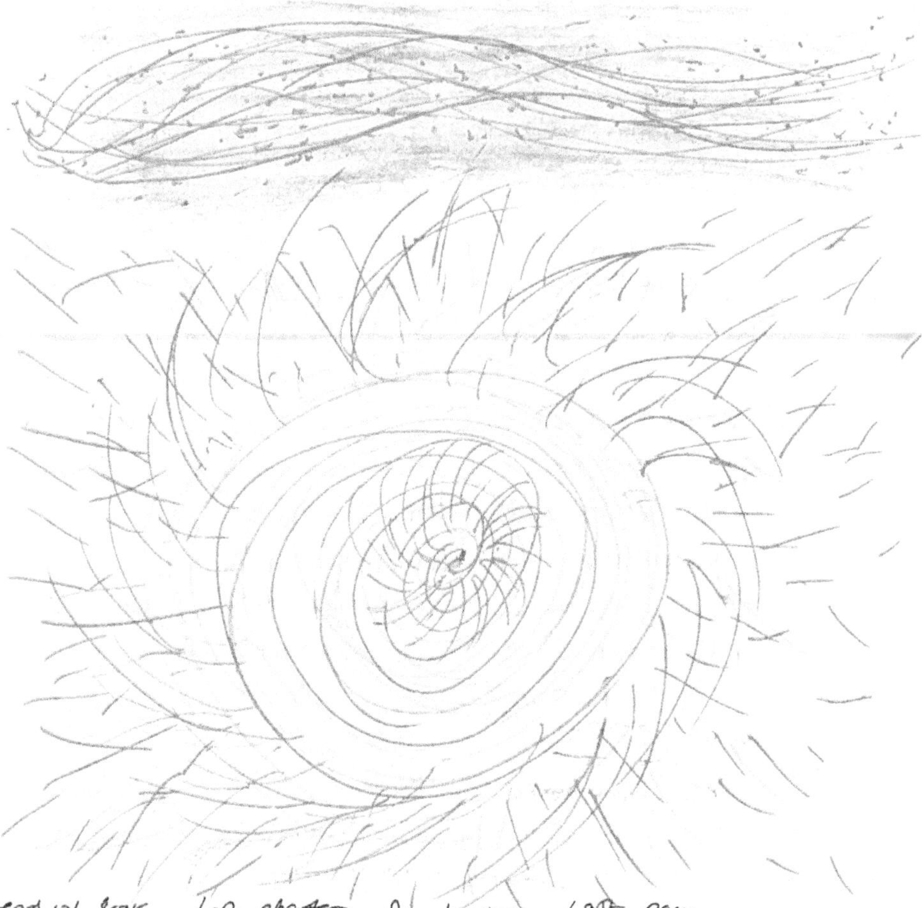

end of book Last chapter Steve Jenkins Last page.

CHAPTER 14

Going Home – Letting go...

Now then this is where things end, as all things do, and new things begin...

Nothing in our world or the universe stays the same.
Everything must change and nothing lives forever: plants, flowers, birds, bees, animals and humans.
Everything must make way for the new to begin.
Everything dies eventually.

Now this not scary. It's just Nature's way of allowing a fresh start all shiny and new, how wonderful! How clever is Nature.

Let's look at the life cycle of a humble leaf. The leaf on a tree starts out as a bud, then changes to a brightly colored green leaf slowly growing darker as it ages through our Summer months. When Autumn arrives the leaf changes colour to glorious shades of red, gold, yellow, orange and amber. The leaf is approaching the end of its life. Finally, Winter comes and the leaf falls to the ground brown and dry. The leaf is still very important and useful as it turns to rich soil and helps feed the bugs and creatures. Some creatures store dry leaves to make a warm cozy bed to sleep on during the cold, long winter nights. In Winter creatures hibernate and this helps them survive. The tree is busy making new buds for leaves to appear all over again in the Spring. When Spring arrives it brings hope and new life begins.

What, you may wonder, have leaves got to do with our Bob? Well now here we are as we end our story.

On a beautiful summer day Bob lay in his beloved garden in the cool shade under the apple tree. Bob was very tired and old. He was in his Winter years. Bob's bones ached badly and his heart had beat trillions of times with love and joy.

Bob's beloved human family cuddled him and loved him even more as they all knew it was Bob's time to leave them. Bob was old and tired - too tired to live anymore in his lovely, furry dog body.

His lovely dog body had served him well but now was his time to die. Very quietly, calmly and peacefully Bob's heart beat got slower and slower; his breathing grew gentle and shallow. Finally, his heart beat for the last time. Bob took his last breath and he breathed out slowly for the very last time.

Death had come for Bob's body. It was not painful or scary but calm, slow and peaceful. When this occurs an incredible spectacular mystery of Nature occurs: the cycle of life and death begins.

As Bob exhaled his last breath he thought:

"I've lived a good life;
I have learnt many things about how to live;
I have been kind;
I have loved others and been loved;
I have listened with my heart and ears;
I have seen how beautiful the world is just by sitting and watching from my own front garden;
I have enjoyed the smallest and the simplest of things, a tasty roast chicken meal, a cool drink of water, a nap under a shady tree, a hug from my family, a walk in the sun and many, many, more things;
I have been important because I have lived.

With these last thoughts, Bob let go of the air in his lungs and his essence of life - tiny molecules, participles, atoms, microns, neon atoms - went up into the air high into the sky above and became stardust.

On that Summer's day, the light warm breeze took those little particles of Bob's breath, floating them up into the clouds to fall back down as rain to help Nature water earth. Others particles fell back down to our English garden and settled on lavender in bloom, others on the delicate wings of butterflies and bees, kissing sunny yellow buttercups or caressing the delicate tips of dainty daisy petals. Some particles floated along with the wind roaming here and there travelling to faraway places like:

Japan to see the city of Tokyo.
Thailand to stand with the giant, golden statues of Buddha.
Australia to swim in the Great Barrier Reef.

Hawaii to surf in the highest waves

Africa to play with the big cats on the plains of the Masai Mara and the herds of elephants led by the matriarch (the old wise female in the herd)

Paris to wonder at the twinkling lights of the Eiffel Tower

Italy to hear opera and see the great Coliseum

On and on over the Atlantic, Indian, Pacific Oceans, the Mediterranean and Caribbean Sea.

Flying all around us over the mountains high, the deep blue seas and the green grass in our parks and gardens until Bob's particles, his stardust, fell to earth.

The most important particle, a tiny-micro-minute speck of stardust essence, floated slowly down and swayed on the wind and clouds until it found Mummy-to-be Keelie.

As Keelie breathed in, she breathed in the air and the smells of lavender, English roses, sweet blades of green grass, and a tiny particle of Bob's essence of life – his stardust. This is the mystery and the cycle of life and death.

A new baby was being made just as Mother Nature intended.

We are all part of everything and everything is part of us.

Bob's last breath was the start of something new

And that something new is You

A baby boy named William.

We learnt from Bob that life goes on and people and pets leave us with a legacy from their lives. Remembering those who were important to us, the lessons they taught and love shared with us over the years helps us deal with our own lives.

To miss someone means we had someone or something very good and very special in our life. This is not a bad or sad thing; this is a very good thing! Sometimes people or pets cannot be with us as they should live somewhere else or with someone else and we miss them very much.

If you miss someone or something perhaps you could make a memory book in your mind to take out when you feel sad.

This is our family's memory book for Bob.

Epilogue

Bob's family remembered him with love and laughter. They enjoyed talking about the many memories they shared about Bob. All the family felt they 'carry a little of Bob' with them and of course they do. This is what our memories are; talking, sharing and remembering will help us keep those we love and miss always close to our hearts.

Long before Bob took his first breath there was a stardust baby boy born in 1956. He had a long journey and a difficult birth into the world. Finally he was born late one spring night under the moon, the stars and the sun; the very same sun, moon and stars we all see all over the world.

The baby boy was a very big baby delivered to a very tired mother. He took his first breath and opened his big blue eyes, looking deeply into those of his loving mother and he thought, "So this is where my adventure begins ..."

Lightning Source UK Ltd.
Milton Keynes UK
UKOW07f0214141217
314451UK00005B/36/P